BOWLING
ALI

Written by Connie Amarel
Illustrated by Swapan Debnath

This book is dedicated to everyone who loves the sport of bowling. It is also lovingly dedicated to my beautiful niece and grandnieces Cassie, Madison and Paisley, and to my handsome nephew Jon. Much love and appreciation to my dear friend Alan for his excellent suggestions and valuable input, and to my bowling buddies Brenda, Donna, Gloria, Vicki, Priya, and especially Pam who gave me the idea for this book. With utmost gratitude to my incredibly talented illustrator Swapan whose illustrations bring my books to life in the most magnificent way. To my husband Mike who helps me every step of the way, my daughter Michele, son Chris and DIL Larisa, I love you all so much.

It was a warm and sunny day at Paisley Ranch. The breeze gently swayed the corn in the corn field and you could hear the leaves rustling in the trees.

The owners of the ranch, Jon and Cassie Paisley, woke up early every morning to feed their animals and make sure they had plenty of water.

Jon and Cassie had many animals on the ranch. There were horses, cows, sheep, goats and pigs. They loved the animals and treated them like they were family.

They also had a dog named Brody and a cat named Emily. All of the animals got along well and enjoyed being with each other in the barnyard.

Every animal was special, but there was one particular animal that was exceptional. Her name was Ali and she was a beautiful golden brown Angus cow.

Besides being beautiful she was kind and caring. The reason she was exceptional was because she possessed a very special talent. Ali loved to bowl.

She created a bowling lane out in the middle of the cornfield. Ali used ears of corn for the bowling pins and a head of cabbage for the bowling ball.

The animals on the ranch loved to watch Ali bowl and would come out to the cornfield to cheer her on. She loved hearing their cheers and would pose before each shot.

Ali took great pride in every roll. She made sure she nudged the head of cabbage toward the ears of corn at the perfect speed and angle. She almost always got a strike.

The other animals loved watching her bowl and wanted to learn how to bowl too. Ali patiently showed them how to nudge the head of cabbage toward the ears of corn.

They couldn't knock them all down at one time like Ali did, but some of the animals became very good at knocking down a lot of the ears of corn.

One particular animal named Gloria Goat became very good at knocking down all of the ears of corn. She began to think she was better at bowling than Ali.

Gloria decided to challenge Ali to a bowling match. The winner of the match would be declared the best bowler on the ranch. Ali accepted Gloria's challenge.

Gloria wanted to bowl first. The other animals watched as she nudged the head of cabbage toward the ears of corn. It rolled with great speed, knocking down all of them.

Now it was Ali's turn to bowl. She nudged the head of cabbage at an angle so that it rolled quickly toward the ears of corn. She also knocked down all of them.

Frame after frame Gloria and Ali continued to knock down all of the ears of corn. The other animals clapped and cheered wildly for every strike they both got.

It was the 10th frame and the game was tied. Gloria nudged the cabbage swiftly toward the ears of corn getting a strike. She got another strike in the 11th frame.

Gloria spun around in circles while jumping up and down. She was so excited because she really believed she had become a better bowler than Ali.

Gloria needed one more strike to have a perfect 300 game. She nudged the head of cabbage with great force, making it roll even faster down the lane.

The ears of corn scattered in every direction. Gloria was sure they were all going to fall down but one ear of corn remained standing. She had bowled a 299.

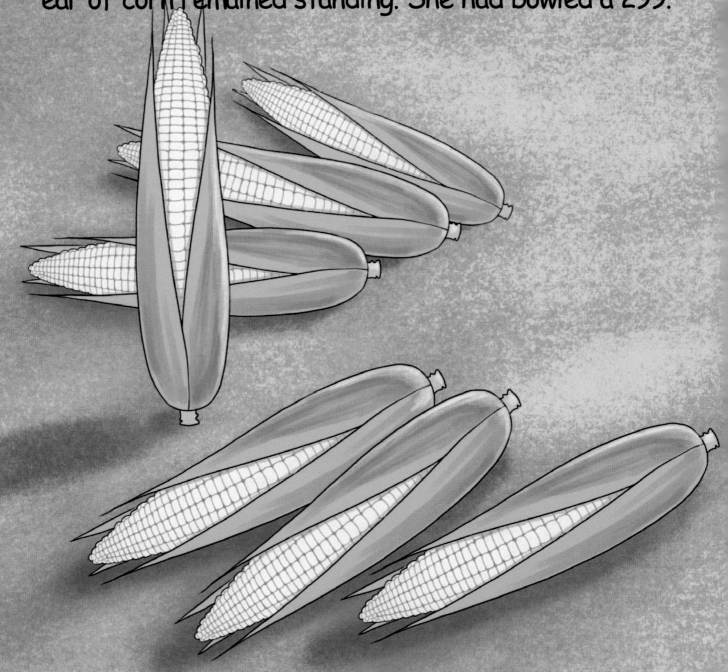

It was Ali's turn to bowl. The animals watched eagerly as she nudged the head of cabbage toward the ears of corn. It was the 10th frame and she needed a strike.

The head of cabbage rolled swiftly toward the ears of corn. It hit them with great force knocking them all down. The other animals all clapped and cheered.

Ali needed two more strikes to win the match. She lowered her snout and nudged the cabbage at an angle toward the ears of corn and again they all fell.

All of the animals watched with anticipation as Ali quickly nudged the head of cabbage toward the ears of corn for her final roll. It hit them right in the center.

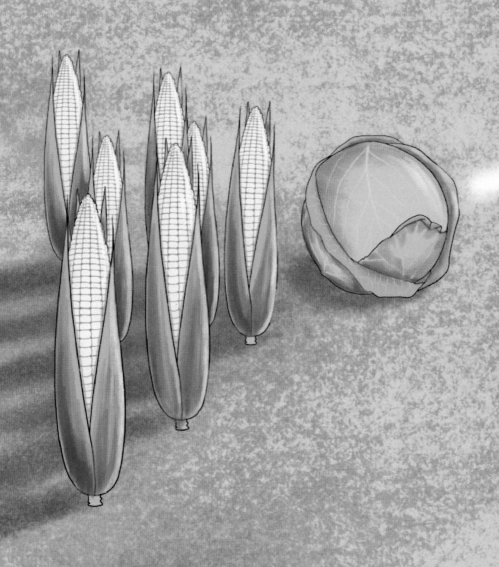

The animals cheered with excitement when all the ears of corn fell. Gloria cheered too. Ali had won the bowling match and was still the best bowler on Paisley Ranch.

Made in United States
Orlando, FL
17 December 2024

56070476R00018